# Fly Away, Young Kalam

Stuti Agarwal



juggernaut

JUGGERNAUT BOOKS
C-I-128, First Floor, Sangam Vihar,
Near Holi Chowk, New Delhi 110080, India

First published by Juggernaut Books 2022



This is a work of fiction. Any resemblance to persons, living or dead, or to actual incidents is purely coincidental.

10 9 8 7 6 5 4 3 2 1

P-ISBN: 9789391165987
E-ISBN: 9789391165048



Typeset in Adobe Caslon Pro by
R. Ajith Kumar, Noida

Printed at Thomson Press India Ltd

*To Myself*

# Contents


| | | |
|---|---|---|
| 1. | Science to the Rescue | 1 |
| 2. | The Dome | 11 |
| 3. | Ready. Set. Go. | 23 |
| 4. | The Verdict | 29 |
| 5. | Off to Camp | 37 |
| 6. | The Rules of Camp | 45 |
| 7. | Challenge No. 1 | 57 |
| 8. | The Launcher | 69 |
| 9. | Lift | 77 |
| 10. | Challenge No. 2 | 87 |
| 11. | Up and Down and Up and Stuck | 99 |
| 12. | Ramanujan to the Rescue | 109 |
| 13. | Challenge No. 3 | 125 |

14. Solar Powered! 139

15. The Final Results 147

Epilogue: Take Off 155

*A Note on the Author* 161

*About Juggernaut Kids* 163

# Chapter 1

# Science to the Rescue

'KALAM!' called out Shankar Mama, the town sarpanch. 'Come see the – what did you call it – the . . . the . . . spider web on this boat.'

'No, Kalam, check the spider web on my boat first!' screamed Murugan Uncle of the Murugan Military Mess. 'I cannot have delays in my spice orders.'

'How can you care about some silly spices right now, Murugan? We're preparing for a cyclone here!' shouted Father Joseph de Mello.

'Yes, Murugan, quit being so selfish!' agreed Pandit Shivaprakash.

The island of Rameswaram was in a tizzy this grey morning in June 1942.

The town had fought many a cyclone over the years, but it had been warned about a particularly nasty one this season and were gearing up for it. 'The kind that was last seen in 1939,' the warning had read.

Ten-year-old Abdul Kalam remembered the terrible time like it had happened yesterday. After all, it was his quick thinking and clever inventions that had saved so many from the angry cyclone and the town tyrant, Punnakai, who had put everyone in danger. But what the boy cherished most was the victory of science and the appointment of his hero, the physicist-cum-mathematician Professor Ramachandran, as vice principal at Vivekananda Vidyalaya and official town scientist.

Three years later, the town was now a big believer of science. There were bits of it everywhere, and Young Kalam was always at the centre of it. Even today, on the day our story begins, he was busy using his latest learning in marine engineering to protect the boats from the cyclone.

'It's called a dock line, Mama, and making a web or criss-cross with it will keep the boat in place,' said Kalam. He examined the boat that Shankar Mama had pointed to before jumping on to Murugan Uncle's boat, his dull shorts, loose, worn-out vest and sandals allowing him a big leap.

'No, no. We have to double the dock lines, Murugan Uncle. Can't be miserly with this. Single lines can break in the cyclone. And let's add spring lines at the front and back,' he continued. 'Yes, that would be best. A thirty-feet spring line should allow a slack of five inches to five feet of tidal movement. A ten-foot range. And raise the lines; we're expecting a higher tide! That should do it.'

Of course, Murugan Uncle understood nothing of what Kalam said. In fact, hardly anyone in the town ever understood Kalam. I wouldn't expect you to either. I can barely ever understand what the boy said! But everyone trusted him blindly.

Kalam, too, was used to the puzzled looks he got. So he picked up the dock lines at once and hopped on to the boat, his pointy nose and wispy hair hopping with him as he tied the line tightly along the length and breadth of the boat.

'Whoheeeeeeeeeeeeeeeeeeeeeeeeee,' onlookers gasped softly at the finished result.

For an island, boats are an important lifeline. Safeguarding them was half the cyclone battle won. And Murugan Uncle's boat now looked like it could survive the worst.

'We must do the same for all the boats,' Kalam thought out loud. 'But I have to go now. I shall be back soon . . . in an hour?'

'Don't worry, Avul. I'll oversee the work

here. You work on your invention. It's an important one, son,' said Jainulabdeen Marakayar, Kalam's father and biggest supporter. Kalam's father was an imam and a simple man with a business of ferrying people to and from Madras of which the island was a part. He was certain his son would do big things, and he made sure to help the boy in every way possible.

'Thank you, Abbu,' Kalam said, giving his father a squishy hug before dashing off to Professor Ramachandran's laboratory.

Tucked away in a corner of Professor Ramachandran's gigantic lab was Kalam's own workshop. It was only a tiny storeroom, but it opened up to a shed. And it was here that Kalam's latest invention stood.

Abbu was right – this was by far the most important invention of his life. It was for a place in a national science competition. Thirty students from around the country would take part in a special two-week camp led by a team of the country's best scientists and engineers.

At the end of it, two of them would get a chance to tour *and* witness the first flight of the Mohawk IVz fighter aircraft, which was being built for the Royal Indian Air Force.

Kalam remembered the first time he had seen the Miles Merlin aircraft in the sky and told his father about his dream of flying. Of course the boy wanted any chance to be as close to an aircraft as possible!

He had been working on his invention day and night. 'A mix of all the sciences,' he called it and revealed nothing more. He even set up a ferocious bark alarm for nosey townspeople. But whatever he was making was growing in size and becoming difficult to keep a secret.

'This should channel all the water into the tank,' Kalam said to himself, sitting down on the step of a ladder to fasten a bamboo pipe on to his invention. 'It must have enough water for seventy-two hours. I wonder if one tank will do,' he thought out loud.

Kalam jumped off the ladder and scrawled something in his diary. 'Hmm, yes, perhaps two tanks, like this, on opposite angles, would be best. Balances the weight too,' he mumbled.

Finally, after minutes of muttering and scribbling, he got up.

'That should do it. Time for biology next. Time to call upon Ram.'

# Chapter 2
# The Dome

In no time Kalam set up the second water tank – a special kind invented by him that inflated when filled to hold up to 250 litres of water and squeezed to the size of a football when empty.

And off he went!

Cycling through Shankar Mama's tamarind plantation–

'Mama really needs to drain out his soil for healthy trees!' Kalam shook his head and picked up a stick to make channels in the soil to let the water out, yet again.

–on to a long sandy seashore–

'That barrel laundry machine seems to be working great, Aunty,' he said, looking over at the string of machines he had designed.

One simply had to stuff their dirty clothes into the barrel and add soap and water. The splashing waves motored the wheels under it to help the barrel rotate along with the clothes, much like the modern washing machine!

–and out near the school, where his best friend, Ram, lived.

Ram's parents were teachers and very strict. Ram was the complete opposite. He was always looking to have fun. Of course, being friends with Kalam meant they were always up to some adventure. Luckily, they also loved studying, which gave the adults little reason to question what the two were up to.

So far they had never been caught. Their parents were certain that their kids were busy studying when they were off testing a new invention, stealing a snack or seeing who could swim farthest with their secret pet, Ramanujan the hen, on their head.

The two even looked almost identical – dark, scrawny and unbelievably nimble – except for their hair, which for Ram were always oiled back, and their clothes, which for Kalam were always stained with one strange substance or the other.

'Ram! It's done. Time for the greens!' said Kalam, rapping at Ram's window.

'But first,' came a voice from inside, 'what is the Copernicum System and who is it named after?'

This was a tradition with the boys. Entry to a room was only allowed on answering a question. The only exception was their friend, Balli, who was let in with a simple secret knock. Balli had recently shifted to a new school to join a better cricket team and barely had time to play. But the three promised to meet at least once a month.

'The Copernicum System is a finding by the Polish astronomer Nicholas Copernicus. It states that the sun is a fixed body at the centre of our solar system and all the planets revolve around it. Before 1543 astronomers believed that the earth was at the centre of the universe,' Kalam said confidently.

The window creaked open.

'Raaaammm!' Kalam said, jumping in. 'I need you, NOW. I have to make the dome green. It needs a balance of plants and critters of all kinds.'

If Kalam was a wizard at physics, Ram was one at biology.

'Everything else is done?' Ram jumped up in excitement.

'Yes, yes, all done.'

'Can we go see it?'

'Let's get the critters and greens first. I'll show it to you when we start planting the dome?'

'Okay,' Ram nodded. 'What about mud and manure?'

'I've already arranged for that from Chandru.'

Chandru was a snack seller famous for his fluffy idlis and mischievous pet monkey, Puttu – not that this is at all important to our story.

'Perfect. Let's go then!'

The two ran off across the island, Ram carefully pulling out plants and Kalam adding them to a large trolley that he dragged.

When they reached the laboratory, the trolley was staggering under the weight of the plants and insects that the friends had collected, including jars full of phytoplankton – 'Ah! To ensure good oxygen levels?' Kalam had inquired as he helped Ram pull out a mesh with the tiny creatures from the shore – and seaweed.

'All right!' chanted Kalam. 'Are you ready, Ram?'

'YES!'

'Okay!' Kalam said dramatically, pulling the cover off his invention.

The glass biodome was sparkling in the light. And with its complex architecture and marvellous collection of inventions –

1. Inflatable tanks
2. Self-defrost glass panels
3. Compost-generated fuel station

4. Self-composting toilet
5. Bath-to-plant water purification system
6. Critter homes
7. Help rockets
8. No-smoke compost stove
9. Urine purification system
10. Emergency oxygen diffusers
11. Extendable rescue rafts
12. Seawater purifier

– it was like nothing anyone could have imagined.

'WOAH!' Ram screamed. 'That's the . . .' He could hardly string his sentences together.

'The biodome!' Kalam completed. 'I like to call it earth on earth.'

'Or Rameswaram on Rameswaram!' Ram shouted, unable to contain his thrill. 'Tell me more!'

'The idea came to me when we received that warning about the cyclone. I decided to invent a safe house. I began making a structure that could be filled with a few days of necessities. But it seemed too small. I told myself to think bigger. And then it came to me. What if I simply made the box bigger!'

'KEEP GOING!'

Kalam was shaking with excitement. 'The dome is the strongest, most stable structure there is, you know. It is aerodynamic, so it can endure winds up to 320 kilometres per hour. It allows for great air circulation inside.

'I've used glass for easy heating and cooling. I've even installed a few smaller inventions to reuse all energy, like this potty that reuses poop to create biogas. And, guess what, since the dome distributes its weight evenly and has a wooden raft floor–'

'THIS FLOATS?' Ram broke in.

Kalam laughed. 'It does! And once we've got the right balance of greens, critters and poultry, this will be a safe house for at least nine people.'

'Let's get to it then,' Ram said, the seriousness of the task finally hitting him. 'We don't have a lot of time left for the selection presentation. The plants and animals have to get used to their new environment, although I'm certain they'll enjoy a nice greenhouse.'

# Chapter 3

# Ready. Set. Go.

The next few days were a whirlwind.

Kalam was so busy finishing the dome that he had begun to live in the laboratory, meals and all.

'A few hours to go,' he muttered to himself, looking at his completed self-composting toilet. 'The cooking area is done. I will add the critters last and . . .'

. . . he dozed off . . .

'. . . oh, the poultry. I forgot to . . .'

. . . and dozed off again . . .

'. . . I wonder if I should add, no no . . .'

. . . and again . . .

The boy had never been this tired.

So tired was he that he was only woken up the next morning by loud knocks on the door.

'Kalam.'

Knock knock.

'KALAM!'

KNOCK KNOCK!

'KALAM!'

KNOCK KNOCK KNOCK!

'KALAM!'

'Huh . . .'

'KALAM, it's Professor Ramachandran. Your mother said you'd be here. I thought I'd come wish you luck. The team has arrived and will be at the school soon. I hope you're ready!' he chirped.

'WHAT!?' Kalam shouted, jumping up. 'I must have dozed off.'

'Kalam, you don't have much time, son. They will want you in the school auditorium with your project in an hour.'

'But, sir . . .'

'Kalam. You know it wouldn't be right for me to bend the rules for you.'

Professor Ramachandran was one of the scientists working on the test flight of the Mohawk IVz fighter aircraft, but since Kalam was competing in the science competition he had opted out of judging it as he wanted to be completely fair. In fact, both Kalam and he had agreed to stop their science projects until the competition was over. They were, after all, teacher and student and best friends combined.

The professor, with his sunny smile, his uniform of a bright, chequered lungi and shirt and his brilliantly white bush of hair, was always a pleasure to be around. Most of his time with Kalam was spent in the laboratory – dreaming, discovering, experimenting, inventing, studying and always having fun. Kalam wanted nothing more than to be like the professor.

'No no, an hour is enough,' said Kalam confidently. 'I was only saying that my project will not fit in the auditorium.'

'Oh!' Professor Ramachandran said in surprise. 'Umm . . . I see. I don't think they've had that problem so far. But . . . umm . . . yes . . . that should be all right. They wouldn't mind coming out I suppose.'

'BY THE SCHOOL SHORE, SIR, IF YOU DON'T MIND,' Kalam shouted

from inside the dome, carefully letting the critters out of their boxes and the poultry into the shed.

'By the shore?'

'I'LL NEED BOTH LAND AND WATER.'

'Right . . . of course. I'll speak to them,' said Professor Ramachandran, his interest piqued. 'I'll see you at the school shore in an hour. Good luck!'

'Thank you, sir!' cried Kalam and got around to the most difficult task of all – preparing the mammoth dome for its ride to the shore.

And what a sight it was!

The mysterious invention towered over the crowd that had gathered to watch as tiny Kalam rolled it out on to the streets and across the town to the school shore.

'GOOD LUCK, SON!' said his parents from the crowd.

'WHAT IS IT?' someone shouted.

'MAKE US PROUD!' some others screamed.

Kalam gave everyone a brave smile, but his heart felt like it would beat right out of his chest as he jumped down on to his stomach to bring the dome to a halt at the shore.

## Chapter 4

# The Verdict

Earth 2.0, as the boys had named the biodome, was a hit, at least with the town audience. The seven judges, all silent through the entire presentation, climbed out of the biodome to the deafening hoots of the townsfolk who had scaled the school wall to watch. Professor Ramachandran was the only one who jumped out loud and gleeful – telling the gathered crowd about his great potty in the self-composting toilet.

'Smell-free too!' he chuckled.

The results would be declared early the next day before the judges went back to Madras.

Kalam came back home very worried. He may have been the cleverest little boy of Rameswaram, but he often lacked confidence.

This time the silence of the judges was enough to make him doubt himself.

It was going to be a long night.

'There's no point sitting here and brooding,' said Ashiamma Jainulabdeen, Kalam's mother. 'There's nothing you can do now even if you don't get in.'

'Yes . . . Ammi,' Kalam mumbled.

'Why don't you go to Ram's for the night? You might want to sit and study for the coming tests instead, Avul – that might come in handy even if you don't get selected. You and Doctor Saheb lose all sense with this science stuff,' continued Ammi.

Kalam's mother could always snap the boy out of his daydreams and even give him a good scolding when needed. But the boy loved her very much – she was the best cook in the world and his most honest critic.

'A sleepover at Ram's sounds like a good plan,' said Abbu. 'And don't fret yet. We must wait to hear from the judges.'

'You're right.' Kalam gave them a hug and left.

The night passed quickly with the two friends filling their tummies with their favourite cuttlefish curry and sneaking off to the laboratory to spend some time in Earth 2.0.

It was well past midnight when they came back to Ram's house. Everyone should have been asleep, but instead the two boys were greeted by their parents and Professor Ramachandran standing at the doorstep, looking at them with a mixture of excitement, anger and worry.

'KALAM! There you are.'

'We've been looking all over for you two.'

'Where do you think you've been, Mr Ram!'

You couldn't tell who said what over the din.

'Said goodnight.'

'I got the result.'

'So late in the night.'

'Some old boat – they had to leave early to make it in time for the train.'

'It came early.'

'Not happy.'

'Thought you were too young. But they couldn't help it – they loved it!'

'ONE PERSON AT A TIME!'

Ram's scream silenced everyone. 'I can barely understand a word.'

'Perhaps a spanking will be easier to understand,' said Ram's mother, looking rather cross with the boys.

As I told you before, the boys had never been caught sneaking out! But it was bound to happen sometime, and today was as bad a day as any other.

'Surely you can excuse him this time,' said Ammi. 'It is a special occasion for the friends.'

'A . . . a special occasion?' Kalam stammered.

'Well, yes! Didn't you hear, you got selected!' said Professor Ramachandran.

'I DID?'

'That's what I've been saying! The judges were worried you're too young for the competition, but they'd seen nothing like

Earth 2.0. Pure genius, Kalam. Their train was preponed so they had to leave today itself, but not before telling me you were in!'

Kalam could not believe it. Almost everyone around him considered him brilliant, but Kalam did not think the same of himself.

'I told you you'd get in . . .' Ammi said.

'That's hardly what you said,' Abbu laughed, poking Ammi in the ribs.

'Oh, do come in everyone,' interrupted Ram's father. 'We must celebrate with payasam.'

'And perhaps Professor Ramachandran can tell us the story again. I heard nothing, as I was too occupied thinking about that spanking from Mummy,' giggled Ram, only to be shut up by his mother's threatening glare.

The rest of the night was filled with bowl after bowl of payasam, laughter and applause as Professor Ramachandran enacted Kalam's presentation onboard Earth 2.0, and the reaction of the aghast judges as he announced that he would like to try Kalam's self-compost toilet. It ended with Ram reading out Kalam's letter of acceptance.

This is to inform you that Avul Pakir Jainulabdeen Abdul Kalam has been selected for the National Science Camp starting 16.07.1942 in Bangalore (find full address on the envelope). Attached is a list of items to be carried by the student and a detailed booklet on the rules of the camp.

Thank you.

But Kalam didn't hear any of it. He was already busy thinking up inventions that would win him a place in the final two!

# Chapter 5
# Off to Camp

It was decided that Abbu would drop Kalam off to mainland Madras. From there the boy would take a train and then a bus to the science camp.

'Here's some adhirasam,' Ammi said, handing Kalam a tin full of the sweet treat. 'Have one a day and share some with your friends too.'

'And here's something to keep you company,' said Ram, handing Kalam a mysterious sack. 'I'm sure you can share some adhirasam with it too.'

'What?'

'Don't open it until you're in Bangalore!' Ram interrupted Kalam. 'And hold on to it tightly.'

'Oh, all right,' Kalam said, wondering what his friend was up to.

'Okay, boys,' said Abbu. 'Time to say goodbye.'

'Go win it!' Ram chirped.

'Remember to follow the rules,' Ammi shouted. 'Be nice to everyone and don't get too caught up in your science stuff!'

'I'll try my hardest!' replied Kalam and waved.

'Be careful, don't talk to anyone on the train. Make sure to check the number of the bus to the institute, it's 867! And . . .' Ammi's instructions continued as the father–son duo sailed off.

The camp was on the outskirts of the city and a long bus ride away from the train station. Add to that a rickety one, and it was well past dinner by the time Kalam reached. Everyone had already gone to bed, which meant that Kalam was left with the last and dingiest bed – in the pantry.

'You'll never go hungry!' Professor Ramachandran laughed, walking into the room.

'Professor!' Kalam smiled.

'Where were you? You were supposed to arrive hours ago! I was about to send someone to look for you.'

'The bus. It broke down a few times.'

'Fault?'

'Loose wiring.'

'Did you fix it?'

'They wouldn't let me. Shooed me away each time telling me that it was not a job for kids.'

'And they said that to you, the meddler!' Professor Ramachandran laughed. 'Well, I better get going. They need me at the laboratory for some testing. I'll see you during meals at least.'

'Okay.'

'All right. Now change and go to bed. You should get a good night's sleep before the big day tomorrow. Sweet dreams!'

'Inventive dreams to you too, Professor,' said Kalam.

Once alone, Kalam looked around his new home. A flickering bulb lit the walls that were lined with countless wooden shelves piled with vegetables, grains, dairy and meat.

In fact, Kalam's bed too was a mattress on a spare bit of shelf.

'*Looks like this bulb too has a loose wire,*' Kalam thought to himself. He would have to fix it in the morning.

He let out a deep sigh. How he missed night-time with his family and sleepovers with his friends!

'Which reminds me,' Kalam said aloud, untying the string on the sack Ram had given to him.

'RAMANUJAN!' he screamed, pulling out the sleeping hen. Tied around her neck was a note. Kalam held it up against the thin strip of moonlight that streamed in through a round window high above.

*Dear Abu,*

*I was certain you'd need a friendly face.*

*Professor Ramachandran made her a few special tonics to help. There was no rule against bringing pets, but it didn't say they were allowed either. I've given her the purple tonic. It puts her in a deep sleep. She'll only wake up if you give her a spoonful of the brown tonic. The blue one makes her clucking silent. There are a few more tonics with instructions on the bottles in case you need them. We couldn't control her egg laying, so you'll just have to find a way to hide the eggs.*

*Good luck. GO WIN!*

*Your best friend,*

*Ram*

*P.S. The yellow tonic is to help her remember her way back to you when you let her out. But it fizzes a lot, so remember to keep it still before opening.*

Kalam gave Ramanujan a spoonful of the brown tonic, and the hen was up the next second.

'Oh Ramu,' Kalam said, hugging Ramanujan. The hen cuddled up to him, and in no time Kalam was in his shelf bed snoring away.

# Chapter 6

# The Rules of Camp

Kalam woke up early the next day and lay in bed, reading the camp rule book out to Ramanujan.

The rules were simple. Time at the camp was divided into three competitions. The first one was a group challenge. The second was a solo task. And the finale had only one rule – every student had to present one invention.

Each student was allocated a total of hundred points – twenty-five each for the first two and fifty for the last one. At the end of the two weeks, the two students to score the highest total would win the final price – a very special tour of the Mohawk IVz fighter aircraft with the scientists, a viewing of its first test flight and a top-of-the-line, professional scientist's toolkit.

'I wonder what the first competition will be.'

'Cluck cluck.'

'Well, whatever it is, I'm sure it will be a lot of fun with some friends.'

'Cluck cluck cluck.'

'It will be like all the times Balli, Ram and I invented things.'

'Cluck cluck. Cooooooooo ....' Ramanujan's clucking slowly went silent as the effect of the blue tonic took hold of him.

'All right, to breakfast then. I'm really looking forward to meeting the other kids and making new friends, all inventors like me!'

As it turned out, the other students – all seniors in school and already part of cliques – didn't look as eager to meet young Kalam. Whispering and pointing followed the boy as he made his way across the mess and to the food station.

'Do you think he's part of the camp?'

'Wonder how he got through.'

'He can't be.'

'I'm sure he's someone's son.'

'Probably didn't even have to invent anything.'

'How can they allow a child in the competition?'

'Don't worry, he'll fail soon enough.'

'What school is he from?'

'Look at what he's wearing.'

'And that satchel!'

'Looks like he's stuffed it with his ABC books!'

'Hehehehehe . . .'

'It's not fair to let in a child.'

But sweet Kalam didn't hear a word of the whispers. He was way too excited.

He greeted everyone and simply went about filling his tray with idlis, neer dosas and chutney, balancing it carefully to a table of boys–

'AAAAAAAAAAAAHHHHHHHHH!'

THAP.

Kalam was lying on the floor, face down, the plateful of idlis and dosas and chutney, all now streaming down his head.

There was a roar of laughter from around the tables. Kalam got up and started brushing his clothes, trying hard not to cry. He felt small and clumsy and stupid.

'Looks like the poor child has fallen already,' a boy at the table laughed.

'Sshh Sridhar,' said another. 'You will get in trouble.'

'What for?'

'For putting your leg out so he would fall,' a girl called out. She towered over Sridhar, looking down at him sternly over her long nose.

'Mind your own business. These are the rules of the camp. He must learn to respect his seniors, not think of them as fellow mates,' said Sridhar.

'I will mind my business if you mind yours,' the girl said, helping Kalam up.

'Geeta, I'm warning you,' Sridhar said sternly.

'You better go and change . . .' Geeta said to Kalam, ignoring Sridhar.

'Don't meddle in this, Geeta. If at all, ensure the boy falls in line.'

Sridhar stomped out of the hall, his friends jogging alongside like security guards.

Kalam craned his neck to look up at Geeta, blinking back his tears. He had never seen such a tall girl!

'I'm Geeta, and this is Kumud,' she said, introducing her friend.

Kumud smiled at Kalam. The two friends looked very different from each other. Geeta was tall and terrifying with a no-nonsense scowl. Kumud was shorter, with a calm air about her. The only thing the two seemed to share were their long kurta pyjamas and longer French braids.

'Hello, I'm Avul Pakir Jainulabdeen Abdul Kalam.'

'Are you part of the competition . . . umm . . . Pakir?' asked Kumud.

'You can call me Kalam. And yes.'

'Oh!' the girls said in surprise.

'Aren't you part of it too?'

'Well, yes we are. But I didn't know they

were letting . . . *kids* . . . participate in the competition,' Kumud hesitated.

'I think it simply said school students in the selection rules,' Kalam said innocently.

'Right. Of course. Well, you might want to go change. The bell for class should–'

TRRRRRIIIIIIIIIINNNNNNNNNNG!

A loud metal bell interrupted them.

'GET UP, KIDS. TIME FOR THE FIRST SESSION,' an old, rather tiny lady, with a squeaky voice to match, shouted.

'Who's that?' Kalam asked the girls.

'That's the camp matron, Farzana ma'am. You better hurry,' Geeta said.

'I–'

The two girls ran off before Kalam could get another word in.

'COME ON NOW, HURRY UP!'

'Ah, you must be the boy who arrived late yesterday,' she said, walking over to Kalam, her stiff cotton sari hiding her feet, making it look as if she was floating towards him.

'Good morning, ma'am. I'm Kalam.'

'Kalam. Hmm. You should know, I do not tolerate tardy kids. Or dirty ones,' she said, scanning Kalam from head to toe. 'And I DEFINITELY don't tolerate indiscipline in my camp.'

'But, Farzana ma'am, I . . .'

'Now, what's the reason for your present messy self?'

'I . . . I fell . . . with my plate.'

'Another rule you might want to remember. No excuses.'

'I really fell. I'm not making an excuse.'

'And how did you fall?' she hissed.

'Umm.'

'How, boy? Tell me now.'

'I . . . I tripped.'

'Here's another rule. You cannot trip in my camp.'

Farzana ma'am seemed to have a rule for everything.

'But I didn't trip on my own. Someone . . .' Kalam began and caught himself.

'I see. Give me a name then.'

'Umm.'

'Are you lying?'

'No.'

'Name then.'

'Sh . . . s . . .'

'Come on, cough it up, kid.'

'Sridhar.'

'Hmm. Now off you go, change and then to Lab No. 5. You have three minutes to class.'

'Yes . . . yes, ma'am.'

Kalam hurried off, hoping the rest of the day would be easier.

# Chapter 7
# Challenge No. 1

The camp was set up in an enormous facility used for all kinds of scientific inventions. This time it was the Mohawk IVz, which was being fine-tuned somewhere out on the grounds away from the busy offices and labs. This meant that only a few rooms were available for the competition.

Storage rooms and corridors had been turned into dorms and out-of-service labs had become classrooms. The students had to fight for standing room, let alone the best seats.

Of course, this wasn't a problem for Kalam, who was so tiny that he could fit anywhere. Even in Lab No. 5, he fit right under the wall-to-wall marble counter while the rest of the students fought for space to stand.

'I am sure you all know of the four forces of flight . . .' said an elderly scientist.

The students nodded.

'. . . they are lift, thrust, drag and weight. It is these four forces that we use when building an aircraft like the Mohawk IVz.'

'Consider this Frisbee . . .' he went on, flinging it in the direction of the students.

'WOAH!' the students gasped aloud as they ducked to avoid getting hit by it. Meanwhile, Kalam was down on the floor, busy taking notes. He had forgotten all about Farzana ma'am and Sridhar. Science always did that to him.

'As the Frisbee flew through the air, *lift* held it up. I gave it a *thrust* with my arm. *Drag* from the air made the Frisbee slow down. And *weight* brought it back to earth again,' he said, picking up the Frisbee. 'Lift is created . . .'

He continued to explain the four forces and ended with the laws of motion – all of which,

he said, he learnt in school and still applied in building an aircraft!

'Well, that's the end of my lecture. I am Dr Ali, and I will be your mentor for the first challenge. For each challenge you'll have a mentor along with these seven great young scientists to go to for advice. And now, what you are all here for – Dr Saha?' Dr Ali smiled, gesturing towards one of the judges to take over.

'For the first challenge . . .' Dr Saha began.

The students were divided into groups of three and each group had to pick one of the four forces of flight.

**Challenge:** To make and present an invention based on a force of flight
**Time:** 30 hours
**Materials:** Everything available in the designated labs and grounds
*Note: There are a total of sixteen labs allotted to the camp with a sign on the door to indicate the same. Please do not enter any other labs.*

'Go on now, pick your groups,' Dr Saha announced, leading to a sudden scramble among the participants to find friends and partners who might prove useful.

'Excuse me,' Kalam clambered.

'Here, Bharat. Come here.'

'Can I be . . .'

'One, two. VINEET, JOIN US!'

'Hi, can I join . . .'

'Sanjay, where are you?'

'Hurry up, Anand.'

'Excuse me, I could . . .'

'One, two, three, four. DONE!'

'Excuse me!'

Just as quickly the chaos died down, and Kalam was left standing alone without a group. None of the other participants wanted a *child* in their group.

Kalam had run helter-skelter from one person to the other asking them to pick him, but everyone had pretended the boy was invisible. After two full rounds, Kalam decided to go back to his place under the counter in front, knowing full well that he would find a group.

Now, if you're paying attention and remember your table of three, you'd know that with a total of thirty students, Kalam couldn't have been left without a group. And just as well, Geeta and Kumud stood huddled in a corner.

'Ah, Kumud and Geeta. You can join Kalam for the challenge,' said Dr Saha.

'BUT . . .' Geeta looked cross.

'Good,' Dr Ali cut her short. 'That's all ten groups done. Let's get on then. Come, take a pick of the four forces.'

'And remember, we will be in this room every morning and evening for classes and an hour after to answer any questions. You have the rest of the day for your inventions!' Dr Saha shouted over the chattering of students excited to begin. 'All right, off you go.'

The students began to thin out as one group after another left to find their own secret spot.

'Shall we check what we've got?' Kumud asked once they were the only ones left in the room.

'Lift,' Geeta read from the piece of paper she had picked.

'That's an exciting one!' chirped Kalam. 'We could make so much with it.'

'Well, yes,' Geeta took over, 'and Kumud and I shall come up with an invention by tonight.'

'But I could help!' Kalam interrupted.

'Oh, you don't have to worry about it. We'll help you sail through this one,' Geeta responded.

'But I don't want to just *sail* through. I want to *do* something. I know I *can* do something.'

'Look, Kalam. It's obvious why we were left without a group today. We are the only two girls in the competition and boys don't think we can be just as good as them, let alone better, at science,' said Kumud. She didn't look her friendly self any more. Her smile was gone, and, like Geeta, she had thin pursed lips and stern eyes.

'So, of course, we were stuck with the kid,' Geeta added. 'But we can't risk that by having a child work on our project. You're sweet, but you *are* ten.'

'And we need to prove them all wrong,' Kumud finished her thought.

'But I've been selected for my invention just like you were,' Kalam said, getting upset.

'Oh, I'm sure you are smart, but look around, Kalam, these are the thirty best student scientists in the country. We'll need more than just smart. You could help us of course, but we must take the lead. We just cannot risk our position in the competition with your limited years of learning.'

'A . . . umm . . .' Kalam stuttered. '*Maybe the girls were right. They did have more years of experience,*' Kalam thought. He was so much younger than them. Why, most of them were a whole head taller and were almost grown-ups.

'How about some formal introductions?' Kumud said, interrupting his thought. 'Without boiling sambar on the head.' She seemed to be back to her chirpy self.

'Well, I'm Geeta from Mussoorie, and I am in the eleventh grade.'

'And I'm Kumud. I'm from Delhi, and I am also in the eleventh grade.'

'Umm . . . I'm Avul Pakir Jainulabdeen Abdul Kalam from Vivekananda Vidyalaya in Rameswaram. I'm in the fifth grade.'

TRRRRRIIIIIIIIINNNNNNNNNNG!

'That's the bell for lunch!'

'How about we meet in the lab after lunch and discuss the ideas Geeta and I come up with? We can talk about how to take it forward then.'

'Can I give ideas too?'

'Kalam . . . it will be better to just go with . . .'

'I'll just tell you my ideas,' interrupted Kalam, 'it's okay if we don't use them.' After all, Kalam was an inventor, and he was always thinking of what to make next.

'Sure . . . I guess.'

'In an hour then!'

Kalam dashed off to his room. He had no time for lunch. His mind was exploding with ideas!

# Chapter 8

# The Launcher

'Since we don't have much time, we've come up with a simple chemical experiment,' Geeta announced when the three resumed after lunch.

'We propose a rocket made of sodium hydrogen carbonate and citric acid, which will, when dissolved in water, explode to launch the rocket,' Kumud explained.

The idea was a sound one.

'That's a good idea,' Kalam said. 'Can I go now?'

'One second, we have one more idea. A simple invention – a pull helicopter. We make a simple wheel helicopter that sits on a stick. A twist-up rubber band will rotate the stick, which will create the lift,' Kumud said.

This too was a good idea.

'Umm . . . if I may.'

'Oh . . . okay. Sure,' said Geeta.

'I think both ideas are great, I just wonder . . . I was just wondering, these ideas, they're not brand new. We've all made these in some form or the other,' he said, remembering his pressure rocket from three years ago.

'They don't need to be new,' Geeta snapped at him.

'Yes, Kalam,' agreed Kumud, 'the rules don't mention that they need to be brand-new inventions.'

'They don't, but I just thought. Sorry, I shouldn't have said anything. I like the ideas, I just thought . . .'

'Well, let's see what you've got then,' Geeta clapped back.

Kalam eagerly pulled out a handful of chart papers and a thick notebook that had INVENTIONS, 1942 written on it. He had skipped lunch to sketch out his invention with detailed notes on its building and working.

'What is this?' Geeta asked.

'It is the design of our motorized launcher,' Kalam said, getting excited.

The first chart listed everything that would be required to make the launcher.

Materials needed:

1. Simple wooden wheels – 2 (with a diameter of 3.5")
2. Thick rubber bands – 2
3. Plastic bits – 2 (round, a little bigger than the hole in the wheel)
4. Glue
5. Battery holder – 2
6. Batteries – 4
7. Wire leads – 4 (preferably red and black to mark two power outlets)
8. Alligator clips – 4 (red and black)
9. Motors – 2
10. Wooden blocks – 2 (1.5"L x 1"W x 2.5"H)
11. Wooden poles – 4 (0.5" x 0.5" x 4")
12. Wooden platform – 1 (22" x 8" x 0.5")
13. Wooden planks – 2 (12" x 2" x 0.5")
14. Paper plane – 1 (A4 size sheet)

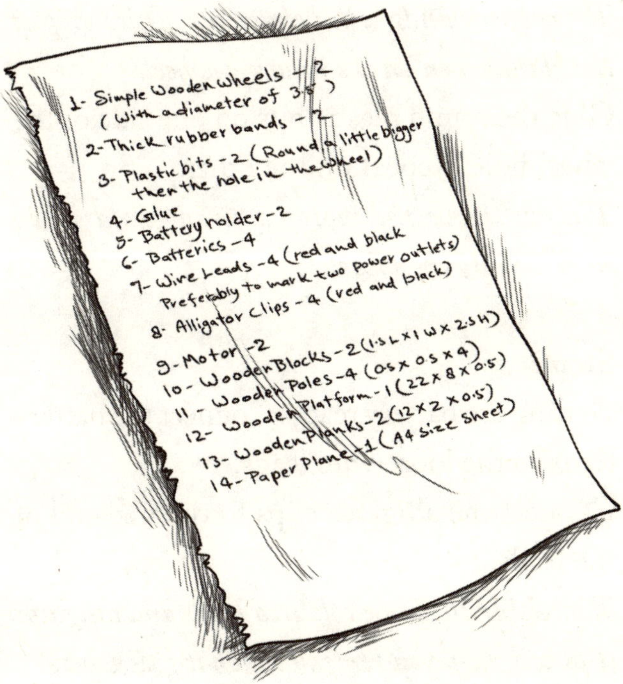


The next three charts were step-by-step notes on the launcher's construction.

**Step 1**

Preparing the wheels: Glue the rubber band around the outside of the wooden wheel. Repeat on the other.

*The rubber bands will help create a nice grip of the plane when on the rotating wheel.*
Glue the round plastic bits on one side of the wheel hole. Repeat on the other.
*This will give the motor a strong hold when inserted into the wheel.*

**Step 2**
Getting the battery ready: Connect the battery leads to the loose wire leads.
Connect the alligator clips to the free end of the leads.
*Tip: Using the same coloured leads and alligator clips will help you remember what goes where.*

There were ten such steps.

The final chart was a diagram of the launcher and its first launch.

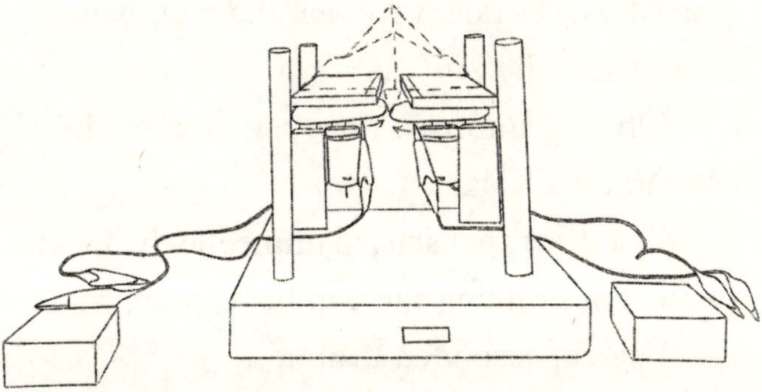

'And all we have to do is–'

'No,' Kumud cut him short.

'What do you mean?' Kalam asked.

'She means that the design is not going to work.'

'But you saw my workings, it's very simple. It will work. And ours will be absolutely unique. We'll surely win with this.'

'Are you saying we can't win with the other two inventions?' Geeta said angrily.

'No . . . no . . . I'm just saying . . . I really think . . . this will be the first of its kind.'

'That won't matter if we don't have the right workings for it. I suggest we go with one of our ideas. We do it very well and win,' Kumud commanded.

'Oh . . . umm . . . o-okay. S-sure then,' stammered Kalam.

'Good, let's get started immediately,' Geeta said. 'I'm thinking the pull helicopter?'

'I agree,' seconded Kumud.

'Oh okay,' said Kalam glumly.

'Let's gather all the materials today. We can assemble it tomorrow before the competition.'

'Will that give us time for a test run?' Kalam inquired.

'We'll see. It should be easy enough. But Kumud and I can draw out the charts today to make sure we get the workings right.'

'All right.'

'Goodnight, Kalam!' the two girls chirped.

'Goodnight!'

# Chapter 9
# Lift

The next day Kalam was busy gobbling down his idlis when Kumud and Geeta interrupted him.

'Hi, Kalam. We were thinking of skipping the morning class to work on the invention

instead. We've finished the charts,' Geeta said.

'Oh! CHOMP. But I don't want – CHOMP – to miss class,' said Kalam. 'I've never had such interesting classes in school before. CHOMP.'

Kalam didn't really like the food at the camp, but he made sure to fill himself up. He had little choice too – he was hungry all the time. Abbu said it was because his brain chomped it all up too quickly!

'We will need time to get the speed of the rotation and the take-off height just right. It should go up at least five feet before it lands,' said Kumud, sounding a little annoyed.

'But . . . I thought you said it should be easy,' Kalam continued innocently.

'Well, yes . . . oh, all right. But we start right after class.'

'Of course!' Kalam quipped, and went back to his idlis.

Luckily for the girls, class ended quickly after a short lesson on the direction of the forces and the equation between them.

*For an aircraft to take off, thrust>drag and lift>weight. To maintain a balanced flight, lift=weight and thrust=drag. For landing, thrust<drag and lift<weight* – Kalam scribbled quickly even as Geeta screamed for him to join them.

The students and judges had cleared out and the three were free to start working on the pull helicopter in Room No. 5.

'I'm here,' Kalam said, 'what can I help you with?'

'We need the charts coloured for the presentation,' Kumud said.

'And paint the launcher for the stick helicopter once I'm done assembling it,' Geeta added.

'Can't I work on making the launcher or the helicopter instead?'

'No, Kalam. Leave that to us. Like we said,

we don't want any mistakes.'

'But . . . right, okay,' said a disappointed Kalam. It looked like he wouldn't be allowed to do anything fun.

He quickly finished the charts and was moving on to the launcher when he noticed that the rubber bands, which were supposed to unwind to lift the helicopter up and out of its launcher, were attached incorrectly. This way the helicopter wouldn't launch at all!

'Umm . . . Kumud,' Kalam called out hesitantly.

'Yes?'

'The rubber bands on the launcher . . . they are not . . . umm . . . correct.'

'What do you mean they are not correct?' Geeta asked. 'I fixed them up myself.'

'Well . . . they are hooked the wrong way. They won't release the helicopter.'

'They're where they're supposed to be, Kalam. Let us handle it,' cut in Kumud.

'But . . .'

'Kalam, we told you to trust us. We've done this for many more years than you. The rubber bands are in their right place,' Geeta said roughly.

'And . . . oh! The lunch bell . . . let's go. Kalam don't look so sad. How about you introduce the group and our invention?' Kumud suggested.

'I suppose . . .' Kalam whispered. How he

wished he was back home inventing with Professor Ramachandran and Ram.

The presentations were held in the garden. And, as Kalam had predicted, it was a competition of chemical and stick helicopters – exactly the kind the girls had suggested.

They all worked perfectly well too, and the presentations were good and almost all the flying objects had a smooth take-off and landing. If only they had gone with the launcher Kalam had invented! But Kalam had told himself not to complain and give his best to his part of the presentation, which was the final one.

'. . . over to my teammate Kumud, who will set off our helicopter, and Geeta, who will narrate the process.'

'Thank you, Kalam,' said Geeta politely. The two had worn a fresh set of kurtas, both blue

to match, and Kalam had made team badges that were pinned neatly to their dupattas.

'You will see that Kumud is winding the rubber band to create tension, thus ensuring a greater lift to the helicopter. That done, she is now going to release in 3 . . . 2 . . . 1 . . .'

The helicopter did not take off, once again as Kalam had predicted.

'Umm . . . one . . . one second,' Kumud stuttered, fiddling with the helicopter.

But Kalam knew nothing would work. They would have to take off the rubber bands and redo them completely.

'Just . . . one . . .' Geeta said, running to Kumud.

'That's enough, thank you,' said Dr Saha.

The judges walked off, leaving Kumud, Geeta and Kalam standing amid smirks and giggles from the other participants. Sridhar was the loudest of them all.

'Expected, no?'

A child . . .'

'And the girls.'

'Well, good for us. Less competition.'

'I knew they wouldn't be any competition.'

'It's not their fault. They shouldn't allow kids *or* girls in such competitions.'

The three heard every word.

Geeta was the only one who cared to say anything back, giving angry stares accompanied by loud 'we'll show you' screams. Kumud was too furious at herself for having judged the boy, which had cost all three of them the first competition. As for Kalam, he was already busy thinking of how he would make up for this loss in the next task.

# Chapter 10

# Challenge No. 2

The next day was a Sunday and a holiday.

Kalam spent most of it in his room, studying and filling in Ramanujan on the events of the past few days. He only got out for meals and even then came back up quickly. Having no human friends was exhausting. No one spoke to him, and Geeta and Kumud were nowhere to be seen.

By Monday, Kalam was happy to be in class and looking forward to the next challenge. So excited was he that he had forgotten all about the results, which were thus:

| Name | School | Class | Group | Marks |
|---|---|---|---|---|
| Sridhar Mohan | Bishop Wool's School, Bangalore | 12 | 1 | 17 |
| Bharat Agarwal | Saraswati High School, Kathiawar | 10 | 1 | 17 |

| Name | School | Class | Group | Marks |
|---|---|---|---|---|
| Umang Joshi | De Paul Douglas School, Calcutta | 11 | 1 | 17 |
| Vinod Tewari | St John's, Dacca | 11 | 2 | 16 |
| Anand Srivastawa | DAV Public School, Bombay | 9 | 2 | 16 |
| Saad Abad | Makinson Boys' School, Srinagar | 11 | 2 | 16 |
| Sandeep Wahi | Poddar High School, Alkapur | 8 | 3 | 14 |
| Ishwaran Prakash | Burn Hall, Hyderabad | 11 | 3 | 14 |
| Aamir Ali | St George's, Karachi | 12 | 3 | 14 |
| Mario Martin | Loyola School, Goa | 12 | 4 | 16.5 |
| Gael Albert | St Mary's, Pondicherry | 10 | 4 | 16.5 |
| Krishna Prasad | Netaji Subhash Vidyaniketan, Mysore | 11 | 4 | 16.5 |
| Vineet Saraf | Kendriya Vidyalaya, Nagpur | 11 | 5 | 15 |
| Ebunyo Sinte | Johnstone School, Imphal | 9 | 5 | 15 |
| Amjad Qadri | St Paul's School, Banaras | 12 | 5 | 15 |
| Mohan Sharma | Government Higher Secondary, Meerut | 10 | 6 | 16.5 |
| Shailesh Bhatnagar | Rajendra Vidyalaya, Jamshedpur | 11 | 6 | 14.5 |
| Himanshu Pawar | Harthan's School, Bareilly | 10 | 6 | 16.5 |
| Azaan Asad | Holy Cross, Chittagong | 8 | 7 | 14 |
| Wanbok Dkhar | Government Higher Secondary, Itanagar | 10 | 7 | 14 |

| Name | School | Class | Group | Marks |
|---|---|---|---|---|
| Balnoor Behl | Nawaz Public School, Aligarh | 10 | 7 | 14 |
| Cheran Dave | Diksha School, Kolhapur | 9 | 8 | 15.5 |
| Ravi Bhil | Kala Gurukul, Indore | 11 | 8 | 15.5 |
| Prabhu Dixit | Kendriya Vidyalaya, Madurai | 11 | 8 | 15.5 |
| Faizan Saleh | DPC Public School, Jaipur | 10 | 9 | 14.5 |
| Raghu Krishna Mohan | St Plant's Senior Secondary, Cannanore | 12 | 9 | 14.5 |
| Tashi Dolma | Dr Grahan Holmes, Kalimpong | 12 | 9 | 14.5 |
| Kumud Chowdhary | Modern High School, Delhi | 11 | 10 | 10 |
| Abdul Kalam | Vivekananda Vidyalaya, Rameswaram | 5 | 10 | 10 |
| Geeta Wadhawan | Welhams Girls' School, Mussoorie | 11 | 10 | 10 |

As was expected, Kumud, Geeta and Kalam were right at the bottom, and yet the boy couldn't help but be overjoyed.

'Ten!' chimed Kalam.

The girls didn't seem as happy to celebrate.

'Psst . . . Kalam,' Kumud called out, sneaking up behind Kalam as he got on his toes to see the results on the class board. She looked like

she hadn't slept for nights. 'We wanted to . . . well . . .'

'. . . We wanted to . . . umm . . . apologize . . . to . . . to you,' Geeta finished, fidgeting with her dupatta. Geeta, who was always so confident and had much to say, was out of words!

'For?'

'For not listening to you. Kumud and I studied your plan last night. It was genius. We couldn't believe you came up with that at your age, and so quickly at that. If only we had listened, we wouldn't be at the bottom, would we?'

'But we got a ten! I was expecting much worse. A ten is good enough. A ten means we can still win!'

'I don't know how,' Kumud said.

'We have two more rounds. We can easily make up. And we can help each other, right?' Kalam asked.

'Oh . . . of course,' said Geeta, sounding surprised, 'if you'd like to work with us.'

'Of course, why wouldn't I? Now for the next challenge,' Kalam said determinedly.

There are a few things that help build friendships – apologizing for your mistakes and working as a team are two of them. As the three entered class, they were definitely friends.

'All right, it's time for me to take your leave now and hand you over to your next mentor, Dr Raman,' announced Dr Ali, leaving the room to a roar of applause.

With Dr Raman, an air of seriousness returned to the room. He was unlike Dr Ali in every way. Tall, stiff and very severe. He looked like someone who didn't think science should be fun.

'In the first challenge, you experimented with air and the forces of flight. In the second challenge, you'll be inventing with water,' he said. There were no greetings or introductions with Dr Raman.

'Pascal's Law states that the pressure applied at one point to a liquid is transmitted evenly throughout the liquid in all directions,' he droned on. 'This is applicable to a liquid at rest and means that a pressure change in one part sees an equal pressure change in all parts of the liquid.'

Again, I recommend you don't worry about all this scientific jargon, unless, of course, you really want to. This is tough stuff. And as I was telling you earlier, I don't understand it to this day, even though I've tried really hard. It's worse when someone like Dr Raman goes on and on about it – it makes me doze right off, just like the students in Room No. 5.

They only woke up when Dr Saha took over to inform them in his shrill voice of the next task at hand.

**Challenge:** An invention based on Pascal's Law
**Time:** 72 hours
**Materials:** Everything available in the designated labs and grounds
*Note: Classes are optional for students who do not have any doubts.*

'. . . and the challenge will be a solo one.'

Before he could even finish, the students broke out into yet another scramble to find their corners in the facility.

Kalam, Geeta and Kumud stayed back in the room.

'You'll find me in the ground at the back,' Kalam said.

'In the backyard?' Geeta asked, intrigued.

'I have an idea . . .' Kalam thought out loud. 'I just wonder if I can make it.'

'Okay, you are worrying me,' said Kumud.

'And me! I still have to make sense of what Dr Raman said, forget thinking up an invention!' Geeta cried.

'Here, you can take my notes from today's class,' said Kalam, handing over his notebook. 'I've added a diagram to explain the law and possibly inspire an invention.'

'Thanks,' Geeta said, looking over the notes admiringly, 'these are great! You're amazing, Aloo, did you know that?'

'Aloo?'

'Kumud and I thought we'd give you a nickname!'

'Sure,' Kalam laughed.

'We should get started now,' Kumud chirped. 'Geeta and I will be working in this room. And thank you again for your notes. I cannot believe you'd give us these detailed notes, with ideas too! How do you come up with so many great ideas so quickly? I take days to come up with a good one.'

'That's because Kalam has only childish ideas, each one worse than the other and all bound to fail,' Sridhar scoffed, walking in. 'He's going to dream up a unicorn tomorrow.'

'Don't you have anything better to do, Sridhar?' asked Geeta.

'Perhaps Sridhar's brain can't come with any ideas of his own and he thought he'd try to steal one of ours,' added Kumud.

Sridhar gave a high-pitched laugh. 'You can't be *that* stupid, Kumud. You wish I'd ever bother inventing one of your ideas!'

Kalam watched the three in silence, unable to say anything.

'That's because you can't invent one of our ideas, Sridhar,' retorted Geeta.

'Well, wait and watch me beat all of you. That should shut you all up,' he said, stomping out of the room.

Kalam's voice returned, 'Umm . . . thank you . . . I . . .'

'The least we can do, Kalam,' Kumud smiled. 'Let's get on with our work.'

The three wished each other good luck and got to work, Kalam zooming off to his room.

Kalam spread out his charts and started on his invention plans.

'For years Pascal's Law has been used to work pumps and jacks, places that require press and pressure, right? So there aren't many ways to use the law,' he whispered to himself.

'So . . . we have to make a smarter version of old inventions.'

'Yes! That's it!' he said, jumping up. 'I use the basic principle of pressure from the water to make a lift that stops at various heights. That way one can use the elevator to clean the windows of the aircraft, or push it to go up to the roof or the rudder.'

For the next few hours Kalam sat and drew the workings of He-Man, the hydraulic elevator. It looked like a lot of work, possibly taking up all of the seventy-two hours, but Kalam was prepared for it.

# Chapter 11

# Up and Down and Up and Stuck

By the end of the three days, Kalam had not only built a grand hydraulic elevator – imagine a tall elevator made from wooden planks nailed together that goes up and down when pressure is applied on the attached hydraulic pump – but also tested it out many times. And every run had been perfectly smooth. The boy had even used the elevator to pluck all the mangoes from the tree in the backyard for a feast with the girls!

He was as ready as could be and decided to have a big lunch and take a nap before his presentation.

Back in his room, Kalam was welcomed by a clucking Ramanujan.

'You're really loud today, Ramanujan. You'll blow your cover if you're so loud! Best to give you a dose of the Silencer.'

But even a dose of the blue tonic, the Silencer as Kalam had named it, did not stop Ramanujan, who took to pecking Kalam instead.

The boy couldn't sleep a wink.

'Okay, you're going out for a walk,' Kalam said, exhausted. He gave Ramanujan a spoonful of the yellow tonic (the one that would help her remember her way back to the room) and dropped her off in the backyard.

With his sleep gone, Kalam got on with revising his notes and forgot all about his pet.

He didn't even pay attention to the hen when she came pecking at him in the backyard as he dragged the elevator out to the garden in front for the presentation.

'I give you He-Man – a hydraulic elevator,' bellowed Kalam, pointing at his elevator. 'He-Man works on Pascal's Law and allows one to reach different heights on point B when pressure is applied on point A.'

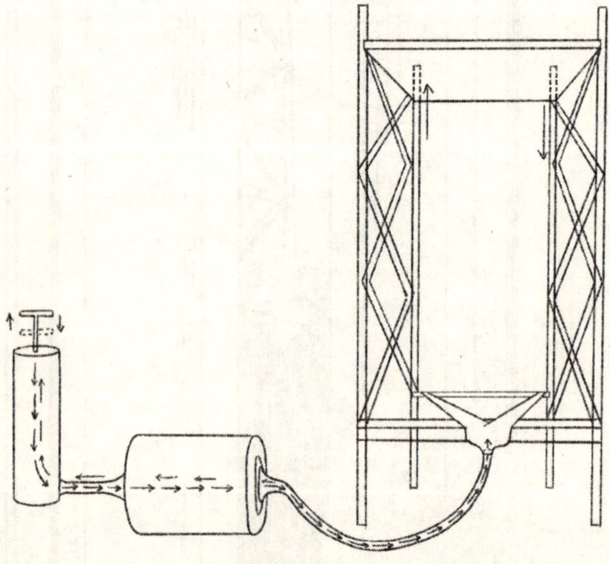

'Let me demonstrate,' Kalam continued. 'Would one of the judges like to volunteer to be on the lift?'

Dr Raman stepped forward. 'I will.'

'Thank you, sir. Now, watch carefully, I will push the lever to point A1 for Dr Raman to be lifted to point B1.'

Kalam pushed down on the handle and up went Dr Raman.

'Now, I will push further to point A2 for Dr Raman to be lifted to point B2 and B3 and B4 and B5.'

Down pushed Kalam and UP
Dr Raman went.

Down pushed Kalam and UP
Dr Raman went.

Down pushed Kalam and UP
Dr Raman went.

Down pushed Kalam and
UP Dr Raman went.

Until Dr Raman was so high up that he could easily jump on to the roof and the judges and students down below looked like small baboons.

'Finally,' Kalam continued, very happy with the result so far, 'all I will do is release the handle for Dr Raman to be brought down to B4, B3, B2, B1 and 0.'

Kalam slowly let go off the handle and down came . . .

No.

Dr Raman didn't come down.

Kalam let go off the handle a little more.

Still nothing.

Kalam tried yet again, with no result.

Dr Raman was stuck.

Kalam dropped the charts and grabbed the handle with both his hands. 'What's happening?' he whispered. 'I don't understand why the lift is not coming down. The handle seems to be just fine.'

There was complete silence as Kalam pulled the handle all the way up in one quick jerk.

But nothing worked.

A loud snigger from Sridhar broke the tense silence, infuriating Dr Raman.

'GET ME DOWN THIS MINUTE!' he screamed.

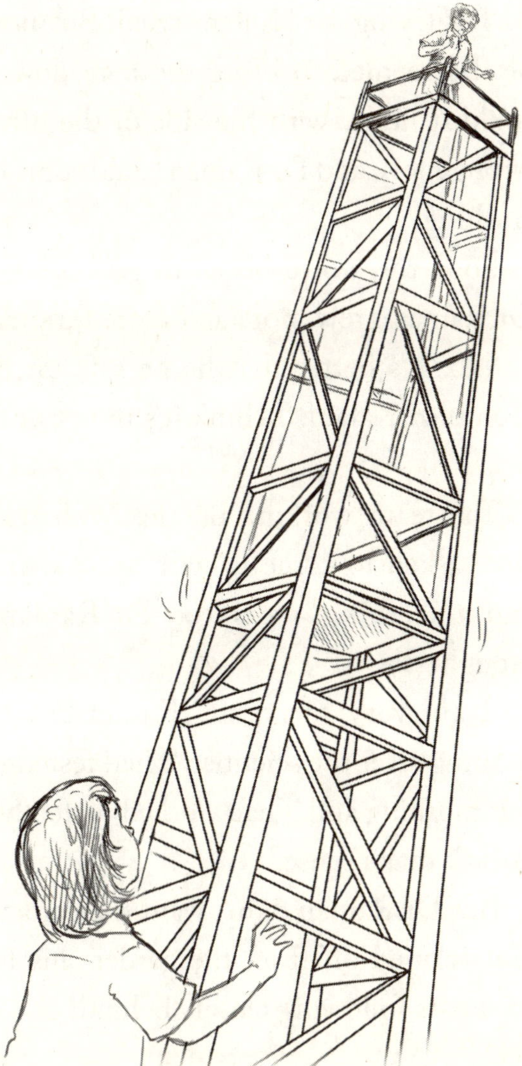

'I'm trying, sir,' Kalam cried. But nothing he did seemed to bring the man down. He couldn't fiddle with the side of the lift. One wrong move and Dr Raman could come down crashing.

Soon the crowd began to get restless, and Dr Raman grew more and more furious.

'No. It's better that he be safe up there,' mumbled Kalam. 'I think it's time to call for help.'

The team working on the Mohawk IVz were asked to come in with their staircases, and a seething, red-faced Dr Raman was brought down.

'I am very sorry, sir,' Kalam cried out, running after the scientist. 'I had tested it just this morning and it had worked perfectly. This doesn't make sense.'

But Dr Raman didn't want to hear a word. He stormed off from the garden, his fellow scientists following closely behind.

Kalam quietly made his way back to his room hoping to escape the evil laughs of Sridhar and his friends, but there he was greeted by an angry Ramanujan.

# Chapter 12

# Ramanujan to the Rescue

Kalam and Ram had adopted Ramanujan three years ago from an old farmer who was giving away his chicks because he suddenly had too many of them. And in all these three years Kalam had never seen her this angry.

'Come on, Ramanujan. I'm upset already, can you stop this and just be nice?'

But Ramanujan refused to stop. She pecked and pecked at Kalam's leg until he shooed her away, which only made her charge in and out of the room, clucking animatedly without a sound.

'What is it, Ramanujan! Why can't you stop!'

When nothing he did worked and Ramanujan continued to purposefully march in and out of the room, Kalam was certain something was wrong. He decided to follow the hen, who took him out and to the dorm room beside the pantry, where some students were busy celebrating. He recognized the voice of Sridhar Mohan.

There he stood silently against the wall – with Ramanujan tucked between his legs – listening as the others in the room cheered Sridhar on.

'Good riddance! That will teach the little brat to snitch,' Kalam heard Sridhar saying.

'Yes, it was a good idea that, blocking the lift,' came another voice.

*'So this is why you've been behaving strange all day. You were trying to warn me!'* Kalam thought, looking at his pet.

'It was brilliant! You should have seen his face when it wouldn't come down.'

The voice broke Kalam's thought.

'And Dr Raman's face too when he was stuck up there.'

'Who cares about Dr Raman?' Sridhar interjected. 'I got the boy like I wanted to. Complaining about me to Farzana ma'am. She gave me a great scolding for it. I had to make the little rat pay!

'They should never have let a kid in. But we need to teach the girls a lesson too. They surely told that boy to complain, and it might also help to have them out of our way. Their latest inventions were good. As was the boy's, you know, but that's obviously nothing to worry about now.'

Fuming, Kalam ran back to his room and banged the door shut behind him.

'Let's get them, Ramu!' Kalam screamed out loud.

'Cluck . . . puck.'

'I can go to the judges, to Dr Raman! Tell them Sridhar meddled with the He-Man,' he said.

'And say what? That Sridhar and his friends blocked our lift so it wouldn't come down?' he countered himself.

'Cluck cluck cluck . . . cluck.'

'How do we prove that it's Sridhar? We can tell them what we heard.'

'Pu . . . puck.'

'You're right. We have no evidence . . . OW!'

Kalam was so loud that Ramanujan had to peck him to keep it down.

'Okay, okay. I know no one is going to believe me if I say that I followed my pet hen to hear Sridhar and his friends talking about ruining my chances of winning and getting back at me for snitching!'

Kalam thought for a moment.

'I can't think of anything! Maybe I should speak to Kumud and Geeta about this one.'

'Cluck,' Ramanujan agreed, and so, once again, Kalam sneaked out of his room to the girls' room.

'HUH!'

'What is it?' Kumud said, jumping up on her bed as Kalam poked her with a pencil.

'Sssshhhh,' Kalam hissed, gesturing for Geeta and her to follow him out.

Once in his room, he told them everything he had overheard.

'We need to get back at the rat,' said Geeta.

The girls were hopping mad.

'Oh, we can do something for sure,' said Kumud, a sly smile spreading across her face. The girls would have been shocked at their introduction to Ramanujan had they not been enraged over what they had just heard.

'What do you have in mind?'

'You're right, no one will believe you without any evidence. But I hear this Sridhar fellow is mighty afraid of ghosts.'

'Okay . . .'

'So how about some ghost rockets to

surprise him in the middle of the night?' Kumud suggested.

'Tell me more,' said Kalam as a wicked smile crept across his face too.

Geeta and Kumud loved having fun with science, just like Kalam did back home!

'Well, we don't need much – canisters, sheets and markers, corn starch and some acetylsalicylic acid. We paint the canisters to look like ghosts and mix the corn starch and water into it. We'll mix the acid right at the end when we place these canisters around Sridhar's bed and run out to watch the show.'

Kalam laughed. 'And we can make some ghost noises from the door!'

'Perfect,' Geeta chuckled.

'But where will we get the corn starch and the acid? Kalam asked.

'Kalam! Your room is a pantry! We'll find some corn starch here. The rest we can find in any lab. And the acid is just aspirin tablets. I'll sneak into the infirmary and see how many I can steal from there.'

The friends waited for Farzana ma'am to complete her nightly rounds before creeping out to collect all the things.

'You two get on with the rest, I'll get the aspirin. It may take some time, since Farzana ma'am sleeps in the infirmary,' Kumud whispered.

Kalam and Geeta nodded in agreement.

By the time Kumud got back, Geeta and Kalam had finished gluing the canisters with white cotton ghosts and were busy mixing the corn starch into the water.

'All clear?'

'Yes, Farzana ma'am was too busy talking to her boyfriend,' Kumud giggled.

'Perfect,' Geeta said, crushing the aspirin tablets. 'Now, how big of an explosion do you want?'

'As big an explosion as one whole asprin tablet would make I think,' laughed Kalam.

That would be a big one!

It was decided that the plan would be executed at midnight. The right hour was crucial for maximum scare, and midnight seemed apt. So, at five minutes to twelve, the three sneaked out, ghost canisters in hand, and a funnel each to make the howling noises.

They would have to crawl in on all fours, pop the tablets in before turning the ghost canisters the right way up and rush out – all in less than a minute, because that's how long it would take for the acetylsalicylic acid to react with the corn starch mix and blow up.

The operation reminded Kalam of the midnight escapade he had carried out with Balli two years ago.

Once at the dorm door he nodded at the girls. They winked back.

They were in and out in about forty seconds, with enough time to make the low booing howls before the ghosts exploded.

Sridhar fidgeted.

'Booooooooooooooooooooooooooo oooooooooooooooooooooooooooooooo ooooooooo.'

Ten more seconds.

'Ooooooooooooo. Ooooooooooooo. Ooooooooooooooooooooooooo.'

The boy on the bunk above Sridhar sat up.

Five seconds.

'Booooooooooooooo. Ooooooooooo ooooooooooooo.'

Four.

Three.

Two.

One.

# 'BOO!'

Whoop!

Whoosh!

Woo!

Whish!

Swoosh!

Whoop!

Whish!

Woo!

Whoop! Whoop!

Whoosh!

Swoosh!

Whirl!

The twelve ghost rockets took off one after the other and pandemonium broke out in the dorm room. There were loud screams and a scuttle to run away from the flying ghosts.

Sridhar was the first to crawl under a bed, howling into a pillow.

Kumud, Geeta and Kalam were rolling on the floor laughing. They were so engrossed in watching the chaos they had caused that they didn't see Farzana ma'am walking towards them.

'OWWW!'

Farzana ma'am knocked them hard on their heads.

'What's going on here?'

'Ouch! Umm . . . we were . . . umm . . . we were woken up by the noise,' Kalam stuttered.

Farzana ma'am! How could he have forgotten that the commotion would wake her up? This after he had made a rule never to get on her bad side! He was sure Ammi would have blamed his excitement for his carelessness.

'Yes, so we came to check,' Kumud continued confidently.

'You are not allowed out of bed after lights out . . . COME WHAT MAY,' ordered Farzana ma'am, pulling the three up by their ears and pushing them into the dorm where Sridhar and some other boys were still howling under their beds.

'THAT'S ENOUGH!' she screamed, bringing the crying to an immediate halt. 'What do you think is happening here!'

'Ma'am . . . there were . . . gh . . . ghosts . . .'

'Whizzing ghosts . . .'

'Whooping ghosts . . .'

'STOP THIS NONSENSE AT ONCE. You are all going to face punishment for this ruckus. Ghosts you say. Back to your beds this instant!'

Luckily for the three friends, she saw none of the ghost canisters that were strewn around the room. But Sridhar spotted them as he crawled out from under the bed. As he turned his gaze from the canisters to the still-giggling friends, he knew at once that the three had been behind the prank.

'Ma'am!' he cried, pointing at the three of them. 'Ma'am, these three . . .'

A stern look from Kumud shut him up. They both understood that it was a well-deserved payback. After all, he was the one who had started it all by tripping Kalam the first day.

'Ah, yes. You will all receive a penalty – twenty-four hours spent cleaning the camp

with me. This includes the three of you,' she said as she turned to Kumud, Geeta and Kalam.

The three friends looked at each other worried. This meant they'd have no breakfast or lunch or tea breaks for the next challenge. But they had to admit, getting back at Sridhar for his foul play had absolutely been worth it.

# Chapter 13

# Challenge No. 3

The results for the second challenge were as below:

| Name | School | Class | Marks | Marks |
|---|---|---|---|---|
| Sridhar Mohan | Bishop Wool's School, Bangalore | 12 | 17 | 17 |
| Bharat Agarwal | Saraswati High School, Kathiawar | 10 | 17 | 16 |
| Umang Joshi | De Paul Douglas School, Calcutta | 11 | 17 | 13 |
| Vinod Tewari | St John's, Dacca | 11 | 16 | 14.5 |
| Anand Srivastawa | DAV Public School, Bombay | 9 | 16 | 15 |
| Saad Abad | Makinson Boys' School, Srinagar | 11 | 16 | 13.5 |
| Sandeep Wahi | Poddar High School, Alkapur | 8 | 14 | 16 |
| Ishwaran Prakash | Burn Hall, Hyderabad | 11 | 14 | 14 |
| Aamir Ali | St George's, Karachi | 12 | 14 | 15.5 |
| Mario Martin | Loyola School, Goa | 12 | 16.5 | 13.5 |
| Gael Albert | St Mary's, Pondicherry | 10 | 16.5 | 14 |

| Name | School | Class | Marks | Marks |
|---|---|---|---|---|
| Krishna Prasad | Netaji Subhash Vidyaniketan, Mysore | 11 | 16.5 | 16 |
| Vineet Saraf | Kendriya Vidyalaya, Nagpur | 11 | 15 | 14.5 |
| Ebunyo Sinte | Johnstone School, Imphal | 9 | 15 | 17 |
| Amjad Qadri | St Paul's School, Banaras | 12 | 15 | 14 |
| Mohan Sharma | Government Higher Secondary, Meerut | 10 | 16.5 | 15 |
| Shailesh Bhatnagar | Rajendra Vidyalaya, Jamshedpur | 11 | 14.5 | 15.5 |
| Himanshu Pawar | Harthan's School, Bareilly | 10 | 16.5 | 16 |
| Azaan Asad | Holy Cross, Chittagong | 8 | 14 | 17 |
| Wanbok Dkhar | Government Higher Secondary, Itanagar | 10 | 14 | 14 |
| Balnoor Behl | Nawaz Public School, Aligarh | 10 | 14 | 16 |
| Cheran Dave | Diksha School, Kolhapur | 9 | 15.5 | 16.5 |
| Ravi Bhil | Kala Gurukul, Indore | 11 | 15.5 | 16 |
| Prabhu Dixit | Kendriya Vidyalaya, Madurai | 11 | 15.5 | 14 |
| Faizan Saleh | DPC Public School, Jaipur | 10 | 14.5 | 16 |
| Raghu Krishna Mohan | St Plant's Senior Secondary, Cannanore | 12 | 14.5 | 15 |
| Tashi Dolma | Dr Graham Holmes, Kalimpong | 11 | 14.5 | 15 |
| Kumud Chowdhary | Modern High School, Delhi | 11 | 10 | 20 |
| Abdul Kalam | Vivekananda Vidyalaya, Rameswaram | 5 | 10 | 12 |
| Geeta Wadhawan | Welham Girls' School, Mussoorie | 12 | 10 | 16.5 |

As expected, Kalam was right at the bottom. With a total of only twelve points, he was way behind everyone else.

'See, kid, you never should have come and played with the big boys,' said a voice behind him as he stood staring at the list. It was Sridhar.

Before Kalam could say anything back, he walked away.

'I am never going to be able to catch up with the others,' said Kalam to himself sadly. 'There goes my chance at seeing the Mohawk IVz. Sridhar was right. I wish I hadn't come.' He could have used a hug; if only his dad or Professor Ramachandran were around.

Challenge No. 3 was mentored by Dr Bose, and he was the toughest of the lot. There were no laws to base your invention on and no guidelines except one – the invention must use a renewable source of energy.

**Challenge:** An invention using a renewable source of energy
**Time:** 144 hours
**Materials:** Everything available in the designated labs and grounds
*Note: Labs will be open on Sunday. For students facing penalty, the time has been reduced to 120 hours. Please report to the infirmary tomorrow (Sunday) at 7 a.m. sharp.*

'This leaves it wide open,' lamented Geeta. 'And a renewable source of energy?'

'That's just a way of confusing us,' said Kumud. 'The last challenge was with water, right? That's a renewable source of energy.'

'As is the sun. Wind. Biofuel,' murmured Kalam.

'Right . . .' Geeta said.

'It might be best to decide the renewable energy you're going to use and then think up an invention.'

'So if you choose water for energy, you can

use it to power an invention that, say . . . grinds some grain.'

'Exactly.'

'Aloo, you know the other day when you said our food has energy?'

'Yes,' said Kalam in a low voice. He didn't feel like his usual excited self.

'So . . . a potato has the energy to power a bulb?'

'Yes.'

'Okay, I think I've got it!' said Geeta. 'I'll see you all in a bit. I'm going to think of how I can blow this idea up.'

'I think I've got it too!' said Kumud. 'I'm going to stick with water and use the ancient science of the water mill to power irrigation.'

'Woah . . .' said Kalam. 'Both of those sound brilliant. I can't seem to . . . no-nothing is . . . I'm absolutely blank . . .'

'Aloo, you can do it. We know you can,' said Geeta.

'Yes, Aloo. I'm sure you can catch up. You're brilliant, you are! Look at the notes you've taken and all your ideas. The He-Man was genius. You know you would have won that round had Sridhar not interfered. You must believe in yourself,' added Kumud.

'I bet you would have been on top in the first round had it not been for us. We aren't going to let you give up now.'

'It's fifty marks, Aloo. This is where you can catch up and win.'

'But . . . we lost a whole day. And even if I did invent something great, the others will too.'

'Well, then we just have to make sure that you create something incredible and get those fifty marks. You can't not try.'

'I-I suppose.'

'Yes! Now tell us if you have an idea you want to work on, and we'll help you with it.'

'No, no, Kumud,' said Kalam, 'you should work on your inventions. You two definitely have a fighting chance for that prize.'

'You have a fighting chance too! Don't believe what Sridhar says.'

'How about we meet in the evening for dinner and discuss our progress?' Kalam suggested, wanting nothing more than to be alone.

'Oh, okay,' said Geeta, giving Kumud a nod.

'Sure,' Kumud agreed. 'But you really can do this, Aloo.'

Kalam nodded glumly.

'See you at dinner then!' The two girls bid Kalam goodbye and went their way.

Kalam plonked himself on his plank bed, Ramanujan tucked by his side.

'It's pointless, Ramu. I can't win now. Why should I even bother making anything for the third challenge?'

'Because you are an inventor, Kalam,' a voice came from the door.

It was Professor Ramachandran.

'I came here as soon as I found out about the results. And on the way, I met the girls . . . they told me they were worried about you.'

Kalam looked up at the man he wanted to be when he grew up.

'But Profe–'

'No excuses, Kalam. You are going to finish the next challenge because that's what a scientist does.'

The professor sat down next to his favourite pupil and put an arm around him.

'Kalam,' he said softly, 'I want to tell you a story about another scientist. Shall I? You probably don't know the real story, so listen closely.'

Kalam nodded silently.

'Well, this scientist was good. Over the years, he had many successful inventions. Then, on one, he made a mistake that caused a massive explosion in the lab. Luckily the team escaped, but the scientist was all shook up. Maybe he shouldn't be working on actual machines, he thought.'

'He decided to give up his job and go back to the island where he had grown up. There, on that island, he started teaching at a school, and met a kid. A kid with the biggest dreams and the smartest mind he had ever known. But, above all, a kid who reminded him why he had become a scientist.

'It was because he loved invention. And so the scientist resumed his work. Today he's helping build an amazing aircraft. Do you know who that scientist is, Kalam? You've often told me you want to grow up and be like me, but did you know it's because of you that I went back to science?'

He gave Kalam a tight hug. 'We all feel bad about ourselves sometime or the other. But you can either let that feeling bring you down or get up and do something about it.

Now you have 120 hours, and I am certain that is enough time for you to invent something great. You've done it before and you can do it again. You have a chance to win and you have to try. Don't give up, you never do!'

'Yes, you can win!' Geeta chirped, coming into the room with Kumud.

'You really are the best amongst of all of us!' added Kumud.

Kalam smiled at the three of them. He felt scared and excited. He felt like crying and laughing at the same time.

'We believe in you, Kalam,' Professor Ramachandran said, patting the boy.

'Yes, we do!' sang the girls.

'Come on. Now make something that will win over the judges and make those sour boys blow their tops!' Kumud said animatedly.

Kalam could feel his excitement return. He could do it! He must try to anyway.

'OKAY!' he said, jumping up. 'I am going to do this!'

'Good!' said Professor Ramachandran. 'I must get back to the lab before anyone finds me here. I'm looking forward to seeing all your inventions at the end of the week. Now off to work all of you!'

Once the professor and the girls had left, Kalam made a list of everything he had invented so far.

For most of them he had had days, months even. And he always had help. What could he make that could be completed in 120 hours without any help?

He didn't feel like working with water again. He'd used air for the first challenge and compost for the biodome.

*'Solar power, perhaps?'* he thought.

*'How do I tap it though . . .'*

*'Copper . . . obviously . . .'*

*'But what do I make . . .'*

And suddenly it came to him. He didn't know exactly how he would do it, but he knew he'd need every minute he could get, because he had never seen anything like it.

# Chapter 14

# Solar Powered!

To this day I am not allowed to talk about the materials and methods that went into Kalam's last invention for the science camp. There are people out there who will steal it, I'm told, especially now! All I can tell you is *what* he made and that he spent all the 6,960 minutes on it. Of course, he had to take bathroom breaks, and often his friends dragged him for meals, all the while covering their noses because the boy was stinking from not having bathed for six days!

Kalam didn't sleep a wink in all those days.

Even on Sunday, a dark day for the students Farzana ma'am had punished, Kalam stayed up all night working and reported straight to the infirmary at 7 a.m. And when the other students went to bed exhausted from scrubbing the entire compound until it was sparkling clean – Farzana ma'am had planned a solid twenty hours of chores for each student – Kalam went back to work.

'Get some rest, Kalam,' Kumud said, worried about her friend.

'I can't. I have to make sure this one is good enough to get fifty marks. I'll rest on Thursday after my presentation,' he said before dashing off.

It was impossible to pry Kalam away from his invention. The only time he willingly left the lab was when Geeta called him to help out with her potato-powered model stadium and Kumud with her water-powered irrigation system.

And every time he rushed right back. He didn't even have time to talk about his invention. Or perhaps he didn't want to. He wanted to keep it hidden away from any possible mischief until Thursday, the day of the presentation.

That day – the final day of camp and of the third challenge – students, judges, all senior scientists working on the Mohawk IVz and the staff gathered in the front lawns for the presentations. Professor Ramachandran was there too, standing in the corner.

The air was solemn as the students presented their inventions one after the other. They were all great. After all, they were the thirty best school scientists from around the country!

By the time Dr Saha called Kalam to present, the boy was a mix of nerves and excitement.

'Ye . . . yes,' Kalam stammered, stepping out from behind everyone and uncovering his invention.

What was it? A toy car? A trolley? What was that metal board on top?

Everyone tried to decipher what it was that the boy had created. As I said, there had never been anything like it. Even the judges stood up to watch as the boy spread out his workings and stepped into the invention.

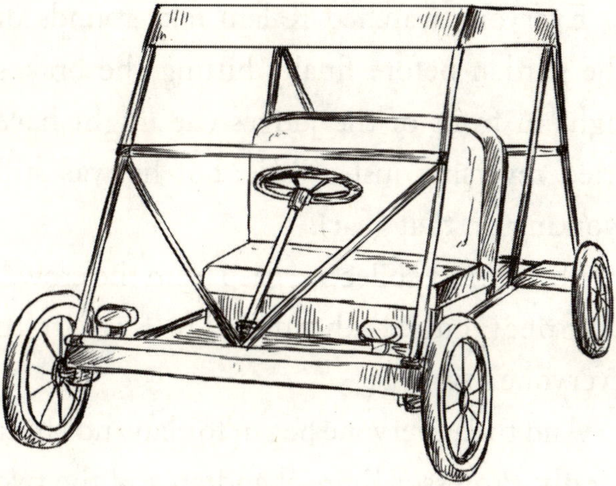

'This,' he said, trying hard to focus on his presentation, 'is Suryonic.'

'Suryonic,' he continued, over loud hoots from Geeta and Kumud, 'is a solar-powered car.'

'A simple push of this button connects the car circuit with the solar panel above and . . .'

Students clapped their hands over their mouths and some others let out a loud gasp. The car – a rough model trolley with a steering wheel and a solar panel roof – was moving, actually moving!

Everyone watched Kalam take rounds of the garden before finally hitting the brakes right in front of the judges (he might have tried reversing just a little, but he was still working on that gear).

There was a collective gasp from the crowd.

'Spectacular!' shouted Dr Raman to everyone's surprise.

And then everyone began to clap and cheer loudly, Professor Ramachandran and the two girls loudest of all. Sridhar was the only one who didn't join in. He was smart enough to know a great invention when he saw one, and he was not happy that it was Kalam's.

The Suryonic was going to be a hard one to beat.

Luckily, Kalam was second to last to be called. The final one was Kumud, who, in all her cheering, had forgotten about her own presentation.

Her irrigation system was an equally great success! She had sneakily installed her water mill system in a stream nearby and laid out the spray system all around the flower and vegetable beds in the garden.

'Now for their morning water dose,' she announced, and turned on a tap that allowed the water to flow through and spray the plants.

'And . . .' she continued, 'something for all the students and anyone else who would like to join.'

With that she bent to turn on another tap that was connected to a fountain right in the middle of the garden!

All the students ran in and began to dance around in the fountain, jumping and splashing each other with water. Even the scientists joined in.

The cooks brought out bowls of chips, vadas, murukku, pakoras and payasam for anyone who needed a quick snack after all the work and play.

The two weeks at camp had been full of fun, friends, learning and inventions, and everyone

was happy to celebrate and forget about the upcoming results. For now anyway.

Everyone except Sridhar, who sat all alone in a corner with a scowl on his face.

# Chapter 15

# The Final Results

Kalam sneaked out of the party. Now that the presentation was over, he could no longer keep his eyes open. All he wanted was to cuddle in with Ramanujan and sleep for hours. And he slept and slept and slept.

He missed tea.

He missed dinner.

He even missed breakfast the next day!

He only woke up when Farzana ma'am came barging in, shouting at the top of her voice.

'WAKE UP, BOY! WAKE UP!'

'Huh?'

'IT'S PAST NINE! ALL THE JUDGES ARE IN CLASS.'

'But . . . that's tomorrow.'

'You sleepyhead,' screamed Kumud, banging on his door. 'Wake up! You've been sleeping for twenty hours!

'YOU! Get back to class. And you, I don't want to see you here when I come back in five minutes. Or else . . .'

'Yes . . . yes, ma'am,' Kalam said. He always forgot about Farzana ma'am and his rule to never cross her!

'Ah Kalam,' smiled one of the judges as he walked in, his hair uncombed and his shirt full of creases. 'Come in, come in, you little Kumbhakarna. As I was saying,' she continued, 'it has been a very hard decision for all of us, but we do have our top two.'

The students waited with bated breath.

'But before we announce the names, I must congratulate all of you for your inventions. We are sure we will see great things in the future from all of you. And . . .'

'I think we should put them out of their agony first, Doctor,' interrupted Dr Bose, laughing. All the judges seemed in a great mood!

'Right right. As I was saying, we have our top two.'

'And they are . . .'

'Oh . . . tell us already!' muttered Kumud.

'Yes, they've been doing this for the last half hour,' added Geeta.

'Then I didn't miss much,' laughed Kalam.

'Sshhh,' shushed Kumud.

'All right, I'll just say it. They are – KUMUD AND KALAM!'

'NO!' screamed Sridhar. 'It's cheating. He knows that Dr Ramachandran! It's all rigged. They couldn't have won. I ruined Kalam's He-Man myself!'

'YES!' Geeta and Kumud screamed. 'We knew it! You're the cheat.'

Dr Bose gestured for the girls to quiet down. 'Sridhar Mohan, please leave the room immediately and wait for the judges in the office.'

Silence returned to the room as Sridhar walked out, his head hanging low. The students later found out that Sridhar was asked to leave immediately and banned from all science competitions in the country.

As for Kalam, he couldn't believe his ears. He had hoped to win, and tried his hardest, but he wasn't sure he could do it. But to have actually won! He didn't believe it when the judges called him to the front of the class to congratulate him, and he didn't believe it when every single student came to shake his hand.

It only sank in when he saw the final result sheet.

| Name | School | Class | Marks | Marks | Marks | Total |
|---|---|---|---|---|---|---|
| ~~Sridhar Mohan~~ | ~~Bishop Wool's School, Bangalore~~ | ~~12~~ | ~~17~~ | ~~17~~ | ~~36~~ | — |
| Bharat Agarwal | Saraswati High School, Kathiawar | 10 | 17 | 16 | 34 | 67 |

| Name | School | Class | Marks | Marks | Marks | Total |
|---|---|---|---|---|---|---|
| Umang Joshi | De Paul Douglas School, Calcutta | 11 | 17 | 13 | 27.5 | 57.5 |
| Vinod Tewari | St John's, Dacca | 11 | 16 | 14.5 | 32 | 62.5 |
| Anand Srivastawa | DAV Public School, Bombay | 9 | 16 | 15 | 40 | 71 |
| Saad Abad | Makinson Boys' School, Srinagar | 11 | 16 | 13.5 | 30 | 59.5 |
| Sandeep Wahi | Poddar High School, Alkapur | 8 | 14 | 16 | 30.5 | 60.5 |
| Ishwaran Prakash | Burn Hall, Hyderabad | 11 | 14 | 14 | 36 | 64 |
| Aamir Ali | St George's, Karachi | 12 | 14 | 15.5 | 38 | 67.5 |
| Mario Martin | Loyola School, Goa | 12 | 16.5 | 13.5 | 33.5 | 63.5 |
| Gael Albert | St Mary's, Pondicherry | 10 | 16.5 | 14 | 28 | 58.5 |
| Krishna Prasad | Netaji Subhash Vidyaniketan, Mysore | 11 | 16.5 | 16 | 34 | 66.5 |
| Vineet Saraf | Kendriya Vidyalaya, Nagpur | 11 | 15 | 14.5 | 32 | 61.5 |
| Ebunyo Sinte | Johnstone School, Imphal | 9 | 15 | 17 | 38.5 | 70.5 |
| Amjad Qadri | St Paul's School, Banaras | 12 | 15 | 14 | 34.5 | 63.5 |
| Mohan Sharma | Government Higher Secondary,Meerut | 10 | 16.5 | 15 | 30 | 61.5 |
| Shailesh Bhatnagar | Rajendra Vidyalaya, Jamshedpur | 11 | 14.5 | 15.5 | 40 | 70 |

| Name | School | Class | Marks | Marks | Marks | Total |
|---|---|---|---|---|---|---|
| Himanshu Pawar | Harthan's School, Bareilly | 10 | 16.5 | 16 | 29 | 61.5 |
| Azaan Asad | Holy Cross, Chittagong | 8 | 14 | 17 | 36.5 | 67.5 |
| Wanbok Dkhar | Government Higher Secondary,Itanagar | 10 | 14 | 14 | 32 | 60 |
| Balnoor Behl | Nawaz Public School, Aligarh | 10 | 14 | 16 | 30 | 60 |
| Cheran Dave | Diksha School, Kolhapur | 9 | 15.5 | 16.5 | 33.5 | 65.5 |
| Ravi Bhil | Kala Gurukul, Indore | 11 | 15.5 | 16 | 30 | 61.5 |
| Prabhu Dixit | Kendriya Vidyalaya, Madurai | 11 | 15.5 | 14 | 30 | 59.5 |
| Faizan Saleh | DPC Public School, Jaipur | 10 | 14.5 | 16 | 26 | 56.5 |
| Raghu Krishna Mohan | St Plant's Senior Secondary, Cannanore | 12 | 14.5 | 15 | 40.5 | 70 |
| Tashi Dolma | Dr Graham Holmes, Kalimpong | 11 | 14.5 | 15 | 35 | 64.5 |
| Kumud Chowdhary | Modern High School, Delhi | 11 | 10 | 20 | 48 | 78 |
| Abdul Kalam | Vivekananda Vidyalaya, Rameswaram | 5 | 10 | 12 | 50 | 72 |
| Geeta Wadhawan | Welham Girls' School, Mussoorie | 12 | 10 | 16.5 | 45 | 71.5 |

'Wow, that's a close margin,' said Kalam to the girls as they stood side by side, looking at the results sheet.

'Only because Sridhar tampered with the He-Man,' said Geeta. She was so happy for her friends. And, between Kumud and her, at least one of them had proven that girls were just as good as boys, and, in fact, better!

But the competition had been very tough, Kalam knew it, and he knew he would have to work very hard if he wanted to become the next Professor Ramachandran.

For now, though, he could lie back and dream about seeing the Mohawk IVz the next morning.

'Not before having a good long bath, you stinky pig,' laughed Kumud, reading her friend's mind.

# Epilogue: Take Off

The Mohawk IVz was a marvel.

Kalam stood staring at it, while Kumud made a sketch of its small, squat body, painted grey and moss green, and its long wings. She even added a pilot in the seat!

To think that this machine would be flying in the air in less than an hour! To think that they were so close to it they could touch it – the thing they saw in the skies!

'Kalam,' Kumud called out, shaking him out of his daydream and signalling him to follow the team of scientists as they climbed on to a platform to take a look inside.

Kalam's heart was beating fast at the sight of the pilot seat and the controls and the thought of the aircraft in the sky.

He carefully listened to every word of the team of scientists as they showed them the engineering of the aircraft, and made a note of everything he saw and how it all worked.

But all the while he was interrupted by a thought. Something that Ram had said. *'Maybe next year they will actually give the winner a ride in the aircraft.'*

They were almost at the end of the tour – after all, there's not much to show in a small aircraft – when the thought turned into an unshakeable wish.

'Psst . . . Kumud,' he whispered. 'I need your help.'

Kumud gave him a questioning look.

'I'm going to hide behind the seat here and go for the first flight. There's just enough space for me!'

'What!' Kumud shouted, unable to control herself.

'Ssssssshhhhh! You'll blow my cover.'

'I think your cover is going to get blown anyway. This is a stupid idea. Do you think no one will notice you're missing?'

'Well . . . the team is busy with the test flight. They will not notice me gone at all. And if they do, I need you to cover for me. Look, we'll be back in half an hour.'

'Aloo, I just don't think . . .'

'Hey, look, they're getting off the platform. Quickly, hide me!'

With that Kalam quickly slid behind a seat and covered himself with a parachute bag. Remember how tiny he was and how easily he could fit anywhere! Kumud was left with no choice but to go after the scientists and hope that Kalam returned unnoticed.

The boy was right. Everyone was too busy with the test to notice him missing, although he could hardly believe his luck.

He kept waiting for the pilots to be interrupted in the middle of the take-off instructions. He waited nervously for an emergency alarm to go off even as the countdown blared on the speaker . . .

But all that followed was the growing whirring sound of the Mohawk IVz as it lifted off the ground. Kalam heaved a sigh of relief as he heard the speaker announce, 'HAWK 1 AIRBORNE.' Now even if he got in trouble it would have been worth it. He would have flown in the sky!

Slowly he lifted his eyes to look up. And there it was – the clear blue sky above. He was flying! The aircraft was flying! Like a bird. He could see the wispy clouds float in and out, hiding the sun and then letting it shine through the glass.

He saw the focused eyes of the pilot as he veered the steering to the left – now Kalam could see a bird really, really high up – and then to the right – now Kalam could see the patchy fields far, far below. Before Kalam knew it, the aircraft was plummeting down, preparing to land.

Kalam closed his eyes. He wanted to remember what he had seen and make a resolution.

*I know what I want to do when I grow up. I want to make things fly. I want to make things that can reach up to the clouds and far beyond into outer space, into the whole universe.*

Now he even had his very own professional toolkit to start with as soon as he got back home!

# A Note on the Author

Stuti Agarwal is a writer (duh!), a self-proclaimed home chef and fantasy-head. When she is not nestled in her couch, dreaming of magical adventures in her hometown of Darjeeling and one day being called Roald Dahl's prodigy, she is participating in pasta cook-offs with herself while listening to audiobooks and practising for the day she wins the Pulitzer. Stuti is the author of several children's books including *The Very Glum Life of Tootoolu Toop*.

# About Juggernaut Kids

Juggernaut Kids is an exciting new imprint for Indian children which focuses on inspiring non-fiction, classic fiction and beautiful illustrations. We want to create great Indian stories for today's child.

## Also in the Young Kalam Series

ISBN 9789386228888
192 pp
Rs 199
B/PB

## Read Stuti Agarwal's Other Books

ISBN 9789386228611
80 pp
Rs 199
A/PLC

ISBN 9789353451431
228 pp
Rs 199
B/PB

ISBN 9789353451547
200 pp
Rs 199
B/PB